APR - - 1999

LI-j

CAN YOU GUESS
WHERE WE'RE GOING?

by Elvira Woodruff
illustrated by Cynthia Fisher

Holiday House/New York

In memory of Crescenzo, master of adventure.
E.W.

To my mother, Louise Wiedman, librarian extraordinaire.
C.F.

Text copyright © 1998 by Elvira Woodruff
Illustrations copyright © 1998 by Cynthia Fisher
ALL RIGHTS RESERVED
Printed in the United States of America
FIRST EDITION
Library of Congress Cataloging-in-Publication Data
Woodruff, Elvira.
Can you guess where we're going? / by Elvira Woodruff;
illustrated by Cynthia Fisher. — 1st ed.
p.   cm.
Summary: As his grandfather gives him hints about all the exciting
things they will see, Jack tries to guess where they are going.
ISBN 0-8234-1387-X
[1. Libraries — Fiction.   2. Grandfathers — Fiction.]   I. Fisher,
Cynthia, ill.   II. Title.
PZ7.W8606Can   1998   97-51431   CIP   AC
[E] — dc21

"Today I smell adventure in the air," Gramps announced as he helped Jack into the car.

Jack grinned. He tried to wiggle his nose. "What kind of adventure do you smell, Gramps?"

"Hold on to your hat," Gramps declared. "We are headed for a very exciting place."

Jack reached up and held on to his baseball cap.

"Can you guess where we're going?" Gramps asked. "I'll give you some hints. Hint number one is monkeys."

"Monkeys?"

"Monkeys," Gramps replied. "We'll probably see lots of monkeys where we are going today."

"Is it the zoo, Gramps?" cried Jack. "They have monkeys at the zoo. Is that where we're going?"

"No." Gramps shook his head. "We aren't going to the zoo today. But they do have some very sassy monkeys where we are headed. You might even want to bring a few home with you."

"In the car?" Jack gasped.

"I don't see why not. We've got plenty of room in the back seat," Gramps pointed out.

"Can you guess where we're going?" Gramps asked
as they drove by some very big trees.

Jack looked out his window at all the leafy branches.
"Is it to the jungle?" he asked. "The jungle is an exciting place and
there are monkeys in the jungle."

"Nope," Gramps answered. "We aren't going to the jungle."

"Is it the park?" Jack guessed. "There are good hills in the park, Gramps. The monkeys could run up and down the hills and play on the merry-go-round."

"Nope, we aren't going to the park," Gramps replied. "Besides, merry-go-rounds make monkeys dizzy. And there are only little hills in the park. There will be very big hills and mountains where we are going. Why, we can even bring a mountain home with us if you like."

"A mountain?" Jack croaked.

"I don't see why not." Gramps shrugged. "As long as we tie it down well."

"Can you guess where we're going?" asked Gramps.

Jack shook his head no.

"Okay," Gramps whispered mysteriously. "Here comes another hint. We're sure to see some knights in shining armor where we're headed today."

Jack's mouth dropped open in surprise.

"Is it the museum, Gramps?" he asked. "Are we going to see the armor at the museum?"

"Not today," Gramps said. "We aren't going to the museum today. But we can probably find a knight and some fine castles where we are going. You do know who likes to hang around knights and castles, don't you?"

"Dragons?" Jack whispered. "Will there be a dragon?"

"I'm almost certain of it," replied Gramps. "It might even be the biggest dragon either of us will ever see."

"You're not thinking of taking him home with us, are you, Gramps?" asked Jack in a little voice.

"I don't see why not," Gramps replied. "We'll just make him promise not to breathe fire on my hood. You know how fiery those dragons can be."

"Having a hard time guessing?" asked Gramps.

Jack nodded his head yes. He thought about the monkeys, mountains, and the dragon, and he wondered where he could find them all together.

"Um, it's a hard one," Gramps agreed. "About as hard as a turtle's shell. Which brings me to my next hint."

"A turtle's shell?"

"Could even be more than one," Gramps told him. "Yep, those sea turtles have mighty hard shells. Of course, we can find all kinds of fish where we're going as well."

"The aquarium!" Jack cried. "Are we going to the aquarium, Gramps?"

"No, we're not going to the aquarium today," Gramps replied. "But we will be able to see fish, turtles, and even sharks where we are going. Do you think we should bring home a shark?"

Jack shot Gramps a worried look.

"You're probably right," Gramps agreed. "The sea turtles would be more fun, anyway. It'll be a little tight, but we can probably fit a couple of them right up here in the front seat."

"Sea turtles, right here?" gasped Jack, looking down at the seat.
"Why not?" Gramps winked.

As they approached a movie theater, Gramps slowed the car. "Ah, just the hint I was looking for."

"Are we going to the movies, Gramps? Is that where we are going?" asked Jack.

"No, the theater doesn't open until much later," Gramps replied. His face suddenly brightened as he pointed to the big poster hanging in the theater's window.

Jack looked up to see a ferocious sharp-toothed T-Rex staring down at them.

"We're sure to be seeing the likes of him once we get to where we're going," whispered Gramps.

"A T-Rex?" Jack gulped as he peered up at the dinosaur's pointy sharp teeth.

Gramps nodded his head. "There will be lots of dinosaurs where we're going."

Jack slid down in his seat to hide.

"But that old T-Rex is a feisty one," Gramps muttered. "He might be a little tricky to take home. We'll probably have to squeeze him into the trunk somehow."

Jack closed his eyes. He began to worry that he would never guess where they were going when he heard Gramps's stomach begin to rumble.

"Must be almost time for a snack," Gramps said. "Which brings me to my next hint, cookies!"

Jack's eyes popped open wide. He thought about their favorite cookies and where they always went to buy them.

"The bakery!" Jack called out excitedly, as he sat up in his seat. "Are we going to the bakery to buy some double chocolate chip cookies?"

Gramps laughed and shook his head no. "We aren't going to the bakery today. Besides, have you ever seen a T-Rex at the bakery? But there very well may be some delicious cookies, just out of the oven, where we are going."

"Here we are at last," Gramps announced, as they pulled into a parking lot.

Together the two went up the stone steps and into the big white building. When they came out, their arms were full of books.

As they got back into the car, Gramps turned to Jack. "Can you guess where we're going now?" he asked.

Jack wiggled his nose and sniffed the air. He looked at Gramps and grinned.

"Hold on to your hat, Gramps," Jack declared. "I smell adventure in the air."

Gramps gave his baseball cap a tug and started the engine.

"What kind of adventure do you smell?" Gramps asked.

Jack looked at all the books on the back seat.

"We're going to a very exciting place," he exclaimed. "A place with monkeys and mountains, sharks and sea turtles, cookies and castles, dragons and dinosaurs. We're going home!"